MAY 2017

SandCastle

Rhyme Time

# Don't Sneeze on Skis

Mary Elizabeth Salzmann

Consulting Editor, Diane Craig, M.A./Reading Specialist

ABDO
Publishing Company

Published by ABDO Publishing Company, 4940 Viking Drive, Edina, Minnesota 55435.

Credits
Edited by: Pam Price
Curriculum Coordinator: Nancy Tuminelly
Cover and Interior Design and Production: Mighty Media
Photo and Illustration Credits: BananaStock Ltd., Comstock, Corbis Images, Hemera, Image 100, PhotoDisc, Rubberball Productions

Library of Congress Cataloging-in-Publication Data

Salzmann, Mary Elizabeth, 1968-
    Don't sneeze on skis / Mary Elizabeth Salzmann.
       p. cm. -- (Rhyme time)
    Includes index.
    ISBN 1-59197-785-1
    1. English language--Rhyme--Juvenile literature. I. Title. II. Rhyme time (ABDO Publishing Company)

PE1517.S3525 2004
808.1--dc22

                                                              2004049037

SandCastle™ books are created by a professional team of educators, reading specialists, and content developers around five essential components that include phonemic awareness, phonics, vocabulary, text comprehension, and fluency. All books are written, reviewed, and leveled for guided reading, early intervention reading, and Accelerated Reader® programs and designed for use in shared, guided, and independent reading and writing activities to support a balanced approach to literacy instruction.

# Let Us Know

After reading the book, SandCastle would like you to tell us your stories about reading. What is your favorite page? Was there something hard that you needed help with? Share the ups and downs of learning to read. We want to hear from you! To get posted on the ABDO Publishing Company Web site, send us e-mail at:

**sandcastle@abdopub.com**

**SandCastle Level: Fluent**

Words that rhyme do not have to be spelled the same. These words rhyme with each other:

breeze

seas

fees

skis

fleas

knees

sneeze

squeeze

referees

these

Michele tries to keep warm.

There is a cool **breeze** at the beach.

Jesse's dog does not have **fleas.**

When Josie gets old enough, she wants to sail the **seas**.

Stephen returns library books on time so he doesn't have to pay late **fees**.

Lizzy **skis** with her parents.

Benji and Rich wear pads to protect their elbows and **knees**.

Brian has allergies that make him **sneeze**.

The rules of sporting events are enforced by **referees**.

Lea's dad gives her a big
**squeeze.**

These four kids are each trying to stand on one foot.

# Don't Sneeze on Skis

Mark is happiest when he is on skis.

He does not mind
paying the fees
or being outside
when it's zero degrees.

15

Down the hills and between the trees,
sometimes it is a very tight squeeze.

But Mark always makes it
to the bottom with ease.

He loves to feel the breeze
when he skis!

Then one day
when he was overseas,
Mark caught a cold
and began to sneeze.

Said his friend Louise,
"Mark, stay off those skis
until you no longer sneeze!"

But Mark said, "Louise,
I can do as I please."

And he went to put on his skis.

But with each sneeze,
Mark fell to his knees.

He said, "You were right, Louise!
Never again will I sneeze on skis!"

# Rhyming Riddle

## What do you call sports officials for tiny insects?

Fleas' referees

# Glossary

**ease.** easily and effortlessly

**enforce.** to make sure that rules and laws are followed

**fee.** an amount charged for a service

**flea.** a tiny, wingless insect that feeds on the blood of animals and people

**overseas.** in a country across the ocean

**referee.** someone who enforces the rules of a sport or game

# About SandCastle™

A professional team of educators, reading specialists, and content developers created the SandCastle™ series to support young readers as they develop reading skills and strategies and increase their general knowledge. The SandCastle™ series has four levels that correspond to early literacy development in young children. The levels are provided to help teachers and parents select the appropriate books for young readers.

**Emerging Readers**
(no flags)

**Beginning Readers**
(1 flag)

**Transitional Readers**
(2 flags)

**Fluent Readers**
(3 flags)

These levels are meant only as a guide. All levels are subject to change.

To see a complete list of SandCastle™ books and other nonfiction titles from ABDO Publishing Company, visit **www.abdopub.com** or contact us at:
4940 Viking Drive, Edina, Minnesota 55435 • 1-800-800-1312 • fax: 1-952-831-1632